A Place to Sleep

Written by Jo Windsor
Illustrated by Christine Ross

Bear

3

"I cannot sleep
in a tree."

"I cannot sleep
in a dog house."

"I cannot sleep in a house."

"I can sleep
in a cave."

11

Symbols

Guide Notes

Title: A Place to Sleep

Stage: Emergent – Magenta

DRA - 3

Genre: Fiction

Approach: Guided Reading

Processes: Thinking Critically, Exploring Language, Processing Information

Visual Focus: Symbols

Word Count: 30

READING THE TEXT

Tell the children that the story is about a bear who is looking for a place to sleep.
Talk to them about what is on the front cover. Read the title and the author / illustrator.
"Walk" through the book, focusing on the illustrations and talking to the children about the different places the bear tries to sleep.
Before looking at pages 12 - 13, ask the children to make a prediction.
Read the text together.

THINKING CRITICALLY
(sample questions)
* Why do you think the bear couldn't sleep in a tree or a dog house or a house?
* Why do you think a cave is a good place for a bear to sleep?

EXPLORING LANGUAGE
(ideas for selection)

Terminology
Title, cover, author, illustrator, illustrations

Vocabulary
Interest words: bear, sleep, tree, house, cave
High-frequency words: I, can, in, a

Print Conventions
Capital letter for sentence beginnings, periods